Circus Pony

Do you love ponies? Be a Pony Pal!

Look for these Pony Pal books:

PONY PALS

Circus Pony

Jeanne Betancourt

illustrated by Paul Bachem

A
LITTLE APPLE
PAPERBACK

SCHOLASTIC INC.
New York Toronto London Auckland Sydney

If you purchased this book without a cover, you should be aware that this book is stolen property. It was reported as "unsold and destroyed" to the publisher, and neither the author nor the publisher has received any payment for this "stripped book."

No part of this publication may be reproduced in whole or in part, or stored in a retrieval system, or transmitted in any form or by any means, electronic, mechanical, photocopying, recording, or otherwise, without written permission of the publisher. For information regarding permission, write to Scholastic Inc., 555 Broadway, New York, NY 10012.

ISBN 0-590-86597-8

Text copyright © 1996 by Jeanne Betancourt.
Illustrations copyright © 1996 by Scholastic Inc.
All rights reserved. Published by Scholastic Inc.
PONY PALS is a registered trademark of Scholastic Inc. LITTLE APPLE PAPERBACKS and the LITTLE APPLE PAPERBACKS logo are trademarks of Scholastic Inc.

24 23 22 21 20 19 18 17 16 15 14 13   3 4 5 6 7 8 9/0

Printed in the U.S.A.   40

First Scholastic printing, September 1996

Thank you to Robert Commerford, Vanessa Thomas, Darra Bernstein, and the kids of The Big Apple Circus — Amber Williams, Danielle Giordanano, Melanie Yoxall, Svete Egorov, and especially Katherine Binder.

Contents

Circus Pony

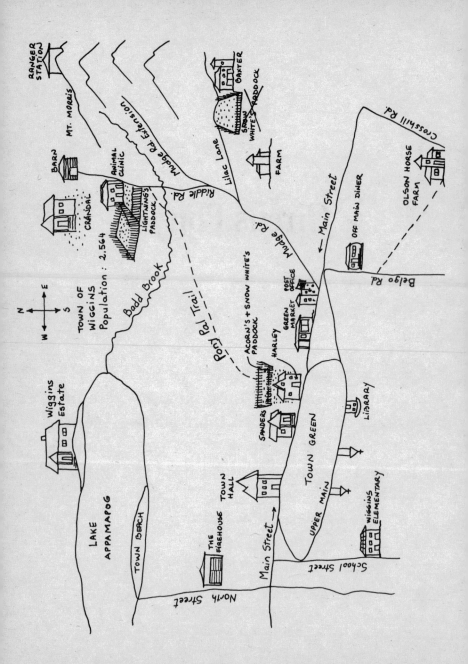

Acorn's First Trick

"Acorn, do you love me?" Anna asked her pony.

Acorn nodded his head yes.

Anna Harley and Lulu Sanders were in Anna's backyard with their ponies, Acorn and Snow White. Anna gave Acorn a small piece of carrot as a reward for doing the trick.

"That's great," said Lulu.

"*You* ask him a question," said Anna.

"Acorn, do you love Snow White?" Lulu

asked. Anna gently tapped Acorn between his front legs with her riding crop.

Acorn nodded his head yes. Anna gave him another small piece of carrot. She gave Snow White a piece of carrot, too.

"Acorn learned that trick so fast," said Lulu. "You've only been practicing with him for a couple of days."

Anna leaned her head against her pony's shoulder. "He's so smart," she said.

Pam Crandal cantered across the paddock on her chestnut pony, Lightning. She came off the trail that led from her house to Acorn and Snow White's paddock. The girls called themselves the Pony Pals and they called the trail Pony Pal Trail.

Pam halted Lightning beside them. "Guess what?" she said. "The circus came in last night. Mr. Olson told my mom."

"But the circus doesn't start until Friday," said Lulu.

"They came early, for a two-day rest," said Pam.

"Let's ride over to Mr. Olson's and see

what's going on," said Anna. "That would be so much fun."

"We can take the shortcut through the woods," suggested Pam.

"Perfect," said Lulu.

The Pony Pals rode their ponies down Main Street and turned right on Belgo Road. They passed Off-Main Diner and made a left onto a woodland trail. Anna and Acorn took the lead. As they trotted along, Anna thought about the circus. She hadn't been to a circus since she was really little. She hoped there would be a horse act. And maybe some ponies.

Anna and Acorn came to the end of the woodland trail and faced Mr. Olson's farm. A big yellow tent stood in a field. The tent sparkled like the sun in a clear blue sky. Anna turned in her saddle and called back to Lulu and Pam. "The circus is here! Hurry!"

The three friends trotted their ponies past Mr. Olson's house and barns and along Crosshill Road.

"Look at all the trailers behind the tent," said Pam.

"That's where the people who work in the circus live," said Lulu.

"There's a fence around the whole place," said Pam. "I guess they don't want people going back there."

"Let's ride around along the outside of the fence and take a look," said Anna.

"We'll have a good view from our ponies," said Lulu.

Pam pointed to a big, blue rectangular tent in the center of the rows of trailers. "They have horses under that tent," she said. Anna could see a long tent with rolled-up sides. She could tell that the space in the tent was divided into stalls. In each stall stood a big brown or white horse. "Those are liberty horses," Pam said.

Anna had heard about liberty horse acts. The horses performed freely, without riders or reins. Their trainers directed them with their voices and arm movements.

"I saw liberty horses perform once," Pam

told Anna and Lulu. "It's like the horses are dancers."

"Hey, I see elephants!" shouted Lulu. "They're next to that silver trailer with the blue stripe."

Anna saw two elephants standing beside the big trailer. One was bigger than the other, but they were both huge. Near the elephants Anna noticed a girl jumping on a trampoline. The girl looked like she was having fun.

"There are lots of kids with this circus," said Lulu. "Look over there."

Anna saw a girl and boy playing kickball. Nearby she noticed a girl playing with a baby in a plastic kiddie swimming pool. Another girl was sitting in a lawn chair reading. And a teenage boy was helping four adults tighten the ropes that held up the tent. Anna also noticed a man juggling tin plates.

Pam started laughing. "Look at that woman on the bike," she said. "She must be a clown."

Anna saw a woman riding a bicycle. Her knees were sticking out and the bike wiggled. Anna kept thinking she would fall, but she didn't. It was very funny. The Pony Pals all laughed.

"It looks like so much fun to be in the circus," said Anna. "Wouldn't you just love it?"

"Not me," said Pam. "I wouldn't want to live in a trailer and have to move around all the time."

"It must be interesting to see different cities and everything," said Lulu. "But I wouldn't want to do it all the time, either."

"I wouldn't mind," said Anna. "I'd love to be in the circus with Acorn. We could be clowns and make people laugh."

"Acorn would make a cute circus pony," said Lulu.

"I have an idea," Anna said. "Let's put our ponies in one of Mr. Olson's empty paddocks. Then we can walk around on the circus grounds."

"They put that fence up to keep people

out," said Pam. "What if someone stops us?"

"Maybe Mr. Olson will tell them to let us in," said Lulu. "The circus is on his land. Would you go ask him, Pam?"

"And tell him we're leaving our ponies in the extra paddock like we always do," added Anna.

"Okay," said Pam. She ran toward Mr. Olson's house.

Anna led Lightning and Acorn toward Mr. Olson's far paddock. Lulu led Snow White. "I'm so glad the circus came to Wiggins," Anna said. She looked over her shoulder at the big yellow tent. "I think that I'm going to love the circus!"

Anna's New Friend

Anna opened a paddock gate and led the ponies in. "Mr. Olson doesn't use this paddock very much," she said. "There will be lots of fresh grass to eat."

Acorn and Lightning nickered as if to say, "We can't wait to eat that sweet stuff."

As Anna took off the ponies' bridles, she thought about her Pony Pals. She knew that Pam and Lulu wanted to have a closer look at the circus animals as much as she did.

Anna had been friends with Pam Crandal since the day they met in kindergarten. Pam's mother was a riding teacher and her father was a veterinarian, so Pam was around horses all the time. The first thing Anna learned about Pam was that she loved horses and had her own pony.

Lulu Sanders had only lived in Wiggins for a short time, but she was already best friends with Anna and Pam. Lulu knew a lot about horses, too. But she also knew interesting things about wild animals. Her father was a naturalist who studied wild animals and wrote about them. Sometimes Lulu's father took her with him on his working trips. Most of the time, though, the trips were too dangerous and Lulu lived with her grandmother in Wiggins. Anna knew that Lulu would want to be sure the circus people were taking good care of their animals.

The two girls put the saddles on the fence rail. "Going to the circus will be a great way to end summer vacation," Lulu told Anna.

"I wish vacation could go on forever," said Anna. "Then we wouldn't have to go back to school." Anna didn't like school as much as Lulu and Pam did. Anna was very smart and a terrific artist. But she was also dyslexic, so reading and writing were more difficult for her. Anna remembered the girl jumping on the trampoline. "I bet the kids in the circus don't have to go to school," she told Lulu.

Pam came running over to Anna and Lulu. "Mr. Olson lent us his passes!" she exclaimed. She handed out the yellow passes. "We have to give them back to him before we go home."

Each pass read GUEST OF THE YELLOW TENT CIRCUS: WIGGINS in big red letters. The Pony Pals clipped the plastic-covered passes to their shirts.

"Let's go to the circus!" shouted Anna. The three friends ran across the field to the circus backyard.

As the girls walked between rows of trailers, Anna looked for the girl she'd seen on the trampoline. She finally spotted her talking to a woman in a lawn chair. The girl noticed Anna looking at her and smiled. Anna smiled back and waved her hand.

"There are the liberty horses," Pam said. "They are so beautiful." Anna saw a young woman and an older man leading the horses toward the yellow tent. There were eight horses of the same height — four brown and four white.

"I bet they're going to practice," said Lulu. "Let's see if we can watch."

Pam and Lulu ran to catch up with the liberty horse trainers. But Anna stopped and turned around to take another look at the girl from the circus. She was surprised to see that the girl was right behind her.

"Hi," said the girl.

"Hi," said Anna. "I saw you on the trampoline. Are you an acrobat in the circus?"

"I'm in the elephant act," the girl said. "I work on the trampoline for balance."

"Wow! Elephants!" exclaimed Anna. "That must be so much fun."

"I have my own elephant," said the girl. "My whole family's in the circus. I'm Crystal Landel. What's your name?"

"Anna Harley," said Anna. "I live here in Wiggins."

Pam waved to Anna from the back entrance of the yellow tent. "Come on!" she shouted. "They said we could watch."

"In a minute!" Anna shouted. Pam went back into the tent. "Are you going to watch the horses practice?" Anna asked Crystal.

Crystal shook her head. "No. I see them all the time," she said. "Do you want to meet my elephant?"

"Sure," said Anna. "I'll catch up with my friends later."

"Let's go then," said Crystal. The girls walked between two trailers.

"Do you live in a trailer?" Anna asked Crystal.

"Sure," said Crystal. "We got a new one

last year. I even have my own room in it."

Anna couldn't believe that she was talking to a *real* circus performer!

Anna followed Crystal around the corner of a big silver trailer. They faced the elephants. "Hi, Elly," Crystal called out. The smaller elephant raised her trunk in greeting. "The fence around them is electric," Crystal warned Anna. "So don't touch it."

The elephant walked toward the girls and stopped at the single-wire fence. Crystal reached up and patted Elly's cheek. "Hi, good Elly," Crystal said. Elly raised her trunk and lowered it toward Anna's feet. "She's going to smell you," Crystal whispered to Anna. "She wants to know where you've walked. That's how she figures out if she should trust you." Anna stayed perfectly still as Elly sniffed at her ankles. It felt like the warm air of a vacuum cleaner. Finally, Elly rolled back her trunk.

"Now you can touch her," said Crystal. Anna stood on her tiptoes and reached up. Elly's skin felt rough and warm.

"Can I give her an apple?" Anna asked.

"Elly will like that," said Crystal. "Hold it out in your open hand."

Anna reached into her pocket for an apple and held it out to Elly. Elly reached over the fence with her trunk and lowered the end of it onto Anna's hand. She grabbed the apple with the end of her trunk and tossed it back into her mouth.

Anna patted the elephant's face again. "It looks like Elly's smiling," she said.

"She is," said Crystal. "She's happy, aren't you, Elly?"

Elly nodded yes.

"Hey," Anna said, "my pony knows that trick, too."

"You have a pony?" said Crystal.

Anna nodded and pointed to the far field where the three ponies grazed. "My friends and I rode here," she told Crystal. "My pony is the small brown and black one. His name is Acorn."

"You're so lucky," Crystal said. "Can I play with him?"

"Sure," said Anna. "You can play with him now, if you want."

"Let's go," said Crystal.

The two girls ran through the circus backyard toward the paddock. Anna hoped that Crystal would like playing with Acorn as much as she liked playing with Elly.

Acorn and Elly

Anna introduced Crystal and Acorn. Crystal petted Acorn. "Do you like Crystal?" Anna asked Acorn. He nodded yes.

"That's terrific," Crystal told Anna. "I didn't even notice you touch him. Do you know how to make him say no?"

"How?" asked Anna.

"I'll show you," said Crystal. Crystal gave Acorn a little scratch on the shoulder. Acorn turned his head to see what had touched him. It looked like he was saying no. Crystal gave him a carrot reward. Then Anna tried the trick. In a few minutes Acorn was shaking his head no when Anna touched him gently on the shoulder with the tip of her riding crop.

"He learns fast," said Crystal. "He'd make a good circus pony."

"He can drive a cart, too," said Anna. "He's been in parades."

"Our circus pony drives a cart in the clown act," said Crystal. She scratched Acorn between the ears. "Can I ride Acorn bareback?" she asked.

"Okay," Anna said. Anna put on Acorn's bridle and reins and lent Crystal her helmet. Crystal hopped up on Acorn's back in one quick movement.

"How'd you do that so fast?" Anna asked.

"It's a lot easier to mount Acorn than it is to mount Elly," Crystal said with a laugh.

While Crystal was galloping around the field on Acorn, Pam and Lulu came up be-

side Anna. "That girl is an excellent rider!" ·
exclaimed Pam. "Look how she's holding
her legs."

"It's easy for her," said Anna. "She's used
to riding an elephant."

Crystal halted Acorn and dismounted as
gracefully and quickly as she had mounted.
Anna introduced Crystal to Pam and Lulu.

"Do you guys want some popcorn and
soda?" asked Crystal. "We can get it free
from the Food Stop."

"Sure," the Pony Pals answered in uni-
son.

The Food Stop was a big trailer that was
like a restaurant. "It's only for us circus
people," Crystal explained. "But you're
with me."

The girls poured their own soda from a
machine. And they each took a box of popcorn. Crystal led them to a big table in the
corner.

Five more kids who lived with the circus
came into the Food Stop. They picked up
their snacks and brought them over to the

kids' table. The Pony Pals met thirteen-year-old Mario Trono, who did an acrobatic act with his mother, father, and uncle. Mario was from Italy, but he spoke English very well. Mario joked around a lot. Anna thought he was funny.

Mario's seven-year-old cousin, Beatrice, wasn't a performer. She lived in Italy, but was traveling with her relatives for the summer. "I learn some English," she said in a heavy accent.

"Your English is good," Lulu told her.

Beatrice smiled and said, "Thank you."

Crystal pointed to the blond-haired girl who was sitting next to Beatrice. "This is Ida Petrovsky," she said. "She's from Russia. Her father is a juggler."

"I saw him practicing," Anna said.

"I am getting a poodle next season to teach," said Ida. "I want to have a dog act. I love dogs. They are easy to train."

"They're not as easy to train as elephants," said Crystal. "Elephants are the easiest animals to train. And they're the smartest." Crystal and Ida had a friendly argument about which animal was easier to train. The Pony Pals smiled at one another. Hanging around circus people was sure a lot of fun.

A boy who looked about nine years old was pulling on Crystal's arm. "You didn't tell them about *us*," he complained. "Our dad's the best act of all."

Crystal gave the boy a friendly push. "This is Charlie," she said. She pointed to another little boy. "That's his brother, Randy. Their mother is the head clown."

"And our dad is the head usher," said Randy. "There wouldn't be a circus without us."

"They're the family with the Shetland pony," said Crystal. "His name is Jumper."

"We didn't see a pony," Pam said.

"Jumper's resting behind our trailer," said Randy. "His leg is a little lame."

"Will he be all right?" asked Anna.

"Mom said he'll be okay in about a week," said Charlie.

"I have an idea. Let's get Acorn and introduce him to Elly!" Crystal told the Pony Pals.

"Is that safe?" Pam asked.

"I know how to do it," answered Crystal.

The four girls took Acorn from Mr. Olson's paddock and led him into the circus backyard. Acorn was on his best behavior and was curious about all the activity around them. They walked him between the rows of trailers toward the elephants. "Now don't be afraid of this elephant, Acorn," Anna said. "She has a very long nose. But she's nice."

"Elly, I brought a new friend to meet you," called Crystal. When Elly heard Crystal's voice, she turned and walked toward them. Acorn made a deep nicker that seemed to say, "Who is this huge creature?" His ears went forward the way they always did when he was afraid.

Anna spoke in a calm, soothing voice as they walked closer to the elephant. When they reached the fence, Elly sniffed Acorn's

hooves with her trunk. Acorn looked up and whinnied. Elly took a step backwards and her ears went out sideways. "Her ears do that when she's afraid," Crystal explained. After a few seconds Elly put her trunk out again. This time she smelled Acorn's face. Acorn took a few steps backwards.

"It's all right, Acorn," Anna said. "That's just Elly's nose. You can smell her, too."

Acorn smelled Elly's trunk and Elly smelled Acorn's back. Their ears relaxed. The next time Acorn whinnied it was a friendly, happy sound. Acorn seemed to be saying, "You look weird, but I like you."

"They're friends already," Lulu said.

"I knew Elly would like Acorn," said Crystal.

Anna was proud of her brave pony and she liked her new friend. She wondered if Pam and Lulu liked Crystal and the circus as much as she and Acorn did.

Mr. Chandler's Idea

The next morning Anna fed Acorn and Snow White their oats. She was putting out fresh hay for them when Lulu came out. Snow White looked up at Lulu and neighed a good morning. Lulu gave her pony a hug.

Lulu began mucking out the pony shelter. "You beat me this morning," she said to Anna.

"I woke up early," Anna said. "I dreamt about the circus all night long. I can't wait to go back there. Maybe Crystal will show us the inside of her trailer today."

"Today Pam's mom is taking us to Danbury Mall," said Lulu. "We're going to buy clothes and school supplies. We've having lunch there and everything. Did you forget?"

"I don't want to buy school supplies," said Anna. "It'll just remind me that school starts next week. I thought we'd all go back to the circus today."

"But we planned this shopping day for a long time," said Lulu. "And then we're going to have a barn sleepover."

"You and Pam go to the mall," said Anna. "I'll go to the circus and meet you later at Pam's for the sleepover. I'll bring food from the diner." Anna's mother owned Off-Main Diner. The Pony Pals loved the food from there, especially the brownies.

"Will you bring brownies?" asked Lulu.

"Uh-huh," said Anna. "And that pasta salad you like."

After Lulu left with the Crandals, Anna rode Acorn to the Yellow Tent Circus backyard. When she reached the electric fence, she looked around for Crystal. Crystal spotted Anna and Acorn and ran over to them. "Let's put Acorn in the horse tent," she said. "There's an extra space at the end."

"How's Jumper today?" asked Anna.

"Jumper will be fine," said Crystal. "He's still resting in a little corral next to the head clown's trailer. Jenny says Jumper's pretending he's lame so he can have a vacation. He does that sometimes."

Anna laughed. "That sounds like something Acorn would do."

The girls put Acorn in the stall. He looked around at all the big liberty horses and nudged Anna's shoulder as if to say, "This is a very interesting place. Thanks for bringing me here."

"Come on," said Crystal. "I'll show you my trailer."

Anna thought the inside of the trailer was the neatest thing she'd ever seen. Crystal's room was tiny, but it had everything she needed. "My sister used to share this room with me," said Crystal. "But she's gone to school in England."

"Where'd she sleep?" asked Anna.

Crystal showed Anna that there was another bed under her bed. "It pulls out," she said.

"It must be fun to drive your house anywhere you want," said Anna.

"I guess," said Crystal. "Come on. Let's go play with Acorn. We can take turns riding him."

The two girls went back to the horse tent. A red-haired woman was looking at Acorn. "Where did this cute little pony come from?" she asked Crystal.

Crystal introduced Acorn and Anna to Jenny, the head clown.

Crystal and Anna showed Jenny how Acorn knew how to say yes and no.

"Can he drive a cart?" asked Jenny.

"Oh, he's great at that," said Anna.

"Could I drive him?" asked Jenny. "We can use Jumper's cart."

"Sure," answered Anna. "That would be fun."

Jenny and Anna hitched Acorn to Jumper's bright red-and-blue cart. Some of the circus kids came over to watch. "Hop in with me," Jenny told Anna. Jenny and Anna drove the cart all over the backyard. Acorn held his head up and trotted with a high step. They made a big circle that ended back at the horse tent. "He's pretty good," said Jenny. "Let's take him in the ring."

Anna and Jenny drove Acorn once around the ring. Next, Jenny told the circus kids to run beside Acorn and make lots of noise. Those kids were so loud that Anna wanted to cover her ears. But nothing could distract Acorn from doing a good job of driving. When Anna halted Acorn, she noticed that a tall man was watching them. The man came over. "Who's this little fella?" he asked.

"His name is Acorn," answered Jenny. "He's a terrific pony."

Crystal introduced Anna to Mr. Chandler. Then Mr. Chandler took Jenny aside to talk to her privately. "Mr. Chandler is the head of the circus and the ringmaster," Crystal told Anna.

Jenny and Mr. Chandler came back to speak to Anna. "The clown pony, Jumper, is resting this week," Mr. Chandler said. "But the clowns like having a pony in the ring. So Jenny and I wondered if Acorn could take Jumper's place while we're in Wiggins. You could drive him, Anna. The people of Wiggins would like to see someone they know in the ring."

Anna couldn't believe her ears. They wanted her and Acorn to be in the circus! "We'll have to get permission from your parents," Mr. Chandler said. "But first I need to know if you'd like to be in the circus."

"Yes. Oh, yes," Anna said. She turned to Acorn and asked, "You want to be in the circus, don't you, Acorn?"

Acorn nodded his head yes and Anna gave him a big hug. "We're going to be in the circus!"

Clown Pony

Anna and Crystal put Acorn back in the stall near the liberty horses. Then they went to meet Jenny at the costume trailer. She was looking through the costumes in a big trunk. Anna and Crystal sat on the floor next to Jenny. "A lot of these things are way too big for you, Anna," Jenny said. "But we'll find something."

Mr. Chandler poked his head into the trailer. "Anna, I've spoken to your parents," he said. "They've given permission for you to be in the circus."

"All *right!*" shouted Crystal and Anna. Crystal put up her hand and the new friends hit high fives. "My friends and I do that all the time," Anna said. "They'll be so excited about Acorn and me being in the circus. I can't wait to tell them."

Anna tried on baggy trousers, short skirts, ruffled jackets, big ties, oversized shoes, and about a dozen different hats. She finally picked out baggy red-and-black checked pants with suspenders, a black long-sleeved T-shirt, a pair of oversized patent leather shoes, and a top hat. "We'll design your clown face after lunch," Jenny said. "But we won't make it a complete disguise. We want the people of Wiggins to recognize you."

Lunchtime at the Food Stop was crowded with the circus people. Jenny introduced Anna to four other clowns. "We'll rehearse with Acorn and Anna at three o'clock," she told them.

After lunch, Jenny helped Anna design

her clown face and showed her how to put it on. Crystal took an instant photo of Anna's face. "It's to help you when you make up for the show tomorrow," she told Anna.

At first, Acorn was a little spooked by Anna's costume and clown face. But as soon as he smelled her and heard her voice, he relaxed.

Jenny hitched Acorn to the clown cart and they drove him into the ring. Next Jenny taught Anna the routine they would do together in the show. They practiced it over and over. At three o'clock, the other clowns came into the ring and practiced with them. The rehearsal was hard work, but Anna loved it. And Acorn loved the attention and the treats he got for being a good circus pony.

After the rehearsal, Anna took off her costume and removed her clown makeup. Then she saddled Acorn for the ride to Pam's house.

Pam and Lulu were waiting for Anna on

the picnic rock. "Acorn and I are going to be in the circus!" Anna shouted as she galloped toward them.

While they put Acorn out in the field with Snow White and Lightning, Anna told her friends about her exciting day. She showed them the instant photo that Crystal took.

"A Pony Pal is in the circus," said Lulu. "This is so much fun."

"All *right!*" the three girls shouted. And they hit high fives.

"Tell us what you and Acorn have to do in the clown act," Pam said.

"It's a surprise," Anna said with big grin. "You'll see tomorrow."

Anna told them more about the circus as they ate their picnic supper. And she showed them the map she'd drawn of the circus backyard.

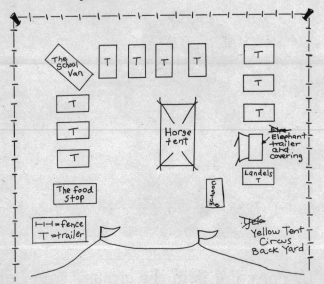

When they finished eating, Lulu said, "We haven't shown you the neat school supplies we bought."

"Let's go to the barn and look at them," said Pam.

The girls cleaned up their picnic things and went to the barn office. Lulu and Pam took their school supplies out of their backpacks. Lulu handed Anna a shiny blue notebook. "Look at this," she said. "There's a pocket folder with each section."

Anna flipped through the pages of the notebook. "It's nice," she said. Then she told Pam and Lulu all about the School Van where the circus kids went to school. "A teacher travels with the circus," she said. "There are just six kids, so it's like having a private tutor all the time. I'd like that kind of school better than Wiggins Elementary."

"Crystal probably wishes she could go to a school like ours," said Pam.

"It must be boring being with the same five kids all the time," said Lulu.

"Circus life is never boring," said Anna.

Fat Cat bounded into the room in three

big leaps and landed on Pam's lap. The girls all laughed. "Life at the Crandals' is never boring, either," said Lulu. Suddenly, Fat Cat leapt from Pam's lap to Anna's lap to Lulu's lap.

"Fat Cat should be in the circus, too," said Anna.

"Fat Cat the Flying Circus Cat!" giggled Lulu. Fat Cat jumped from Lulu's lap and left the room as quickly as she had entered it.

"What'll we do now?" asked Lulu.

"Let's have a checkers tournament," suggested Pam. "The loser of the first game has to go to the house and make microwave popcorn for the other two."

"You guys play without me," Anna said. "I'll watch."

Lulu and Pam played checkers. But Anna slipped into her sleeping bag, closed her eyes, and fell asleep going over her clown act in her head.

Under the Big Yellow Tent

The next morning, the three girls rode over to Off-Main Diner for breakfast. Anna's mother had already told the people who worked in the diner that Anna was going to be in the circus. The cook made the Pony Pals an extra-special breakfast of clown pancakes. The top pancake on each plate had raisin eyes, a cherry nose, an apple slice mouth, and whipped cream hair.

After breakfast, Lulu and Pam rode with Anna to the circus tent.

"We'll miss you on the trail ride today," said Lulu.

"It's the last big one of the summer vacation," said Pam.

I don't care if I miss a trail ride, thought Anna. I'd rather be in the circus. She led Acorn through the circus gate. "Don't forget you're going to help Acorn and me get ready for the show," Anna reminded her friends. "I'll meet you at the horse tent at six o'clock."

Anna and Acorn spent the rest of the morning rehearsing with the clowns. After lunch, Crystal and Anna brought Acorn to see Elly again. This time Acorn's ears didn't go forward and Elly's ears didn't go out. The elephant and pony were glad to see each other. For the rest of the afternoon, Acorn grazed in Mr. Olson's fields and rested. Anna and Crystal hung out in the backyard with the other kids.

After supper, it was time to prepare for the performance. Anna went to the horse tent. Lulu and Pam were already there grooming Acorn. "We came a little early," Lulu explained. "We wanted to have plenty of time to make Acorn look perfect." When the grooming was finished, the girls wrapped each of Acorn's legs in a different color. Next, they went to the costume tent and watched Anna put on her clown face and helped her with her costume. Their last job was putting on Acorn's colorful halter and reins and hitching him to the cart.

Finally, Anna and Acorn joined the lineup outside the tent. They were ready for the opening parade. Pam and Lulu went into the tent to watch the show. Jenny wished Anna good luck. "And remember," Jenny said, "smile and wave. That's how you say to the audience, 'I'm so glad you're here. I'm going to give you my best performance.' "

"Okay," said Anna. But she was so nervous she didn't know if she could smile. When the music started and Acorn trotted into the ring, Anna forgot about being nervous. It was so exciting to be in the circus

ring with all of the other performers. And it was easy to smile and wave at the happy people in the audience. The circus had begun.

The opening act after the parade was The Landels' elephant act. Anna watched from behind the curtain. Crystal made mounting Elly look easy. But Anna knew it was hard. Crystal had to step on Elly's raised leg, grab the elephant's ear, and pull herself up on the big animal's back. Anna held her breath when Crystal went around the ring standing on Elly's back. And she laughed out loud when Elly sat at a table, picked up a bell with her trunk, and rang it. Elly wanted Crystal and Crystal's dad to serve her lunch!

Ivan Petrovsky's juggling act followed The Landels and their elephants. The next act would be the clowns. Anna stepped into the pony cart. "Don't forget," Jenny told Anna. "Big smiles and big gestures."

Anna heard the ringmaster announce, "The Yellow Tent Circus proudly presents its clowns. They are joined tonight by a Wiggins resident, Anna Harley. She's here with her pony, Acorn." The audience clapped as Acorn trotted into the ring. Then the clowns stumbled onto the stage from all directions. The audience clapped and cheered.

Anna drove Acorn toward Jenny and a clown named Rufus. Rufus was doing a crooked cartwheel. Anna pulled Acorn to a halt next to them. She stepped out of the cart and handed the reins to Jenny. Anna demonstrated a perfect cartwheel for Rufus and told him to try it again.

Meanwhile, Jenny climbed into Acorn's cart. Acorn started to walk, then trot. Jenny pretended she didn't know how to drive and that Acorn was running away with her.

Anna noticed that her pony was running away and that Jenny was falling out of the cart. Anna ran across the ring and stopped Acorn. Jenny tumbled out of the cart.

Anna pretended to scold Acorn. Acorn

nodded his head as if he understood every word she was saying.

As Jenny dusted herself off, she noticed a bike nearby. She smiled at the audience and held out her suspenders as if to say, "Here's something I know how to ride." But Jenny wobbled all over the place on the bike. She had as much trouble riding the bike as she had driving the pony cart.

Anna drove Acorn offstage. And that was the end of their part in the clown act. Anna stepped out of the cart and put her arm around Acorn's neck. "You *did* it, Acorn," she exclaimed. "You were perfect. We made them laugh."

When the whole clown act was over, Jenny helped Anna unhitch Acorn from the cart. "You two did a great job," said Jenny.

Anna and some of the other clowns and performers went out front during intermission to mix with the audience. Pam and Lulu rushed up to Anna. "You were as good as the professional clowns," Pam said.

"I was laughing so hard tears were running down my face," said Lulu.

Anna's family came over. "You were terrific, honey," her father said.

Her mother said, "I was so proud of you."

Anna's brother patted her on the back. "Not bad," he said.

"I never could have done that," Anna's sister said. "I'd have been too scared."

A little girl ran up to Anna. She held up a pen and her circus program. "Can I have your autograph, please?" she asked.

"Sure," said Anna. Anna felt famous when she wrote her name.

"Let us see how you did it," Lulu said.

Anna showed the autograph to Lulu and Pam before she handed the program back to the girl.

Anna and Acorn

Pam and Lulu left to get sodas while Anna signed some more autographs. When they came back, Pam and Lulu were laughing. Lulu handed Anna a soda. "Anna, guess who's going around bragging that Acorn used to be *his* pony?" Lulu asked.

"Tommy Rand?' Anna said with a laugh.

"Yes!" Lulu and Pam shouted.

Tommy Rand was a tough, mean-acting eighth grader. When Tommy was younger, Acorn was his pony. Tommy didn't usually like anyone to know he had *ever* had a small pony like Acorn.

Pam imitated Tommy's tough look and voice. "I taught Acorn those tricks," she said in her Tommy-voice. "I could have been in the circus. But Acorn is way too small for me now."

The Pony Pals were still laughing about Tommy Rand when they saw Ms. Wiggins coming toward them. Ms. Wiggins was a great friend of the Pony Pals. She had taught Acorn and Anna cart driving. "I was so proud of you and Acorn," she told Anna. "You were both wonderful."

"Thanks," said Anna.

At the end of intermission, Anna went to the backyard to check on Acorn. She told him all about signing autographs for him. "I'm so happy, Acorn," she said. "There's nothing better than being in the circus!"

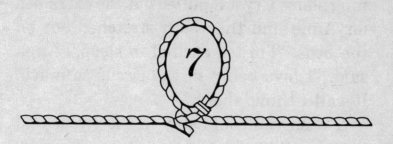

First Star

Anna and Acorn went back to the circus early the next morning. Anna couldn't wait to perform the clown act with Jenny, Rufus, and Acorn again. She was glad that there were *two* Saturday shows.

The audience clapped when Anna did her cartwheels. And they laughed loudly when Acorn ran away with Jenny in the cart. Anna loved that she and Acorn could make people so happy.

After the performance, Anna and Crystal walked to the trailer to rest before the evening show. Crystal pulled out the extra bed for Anna and they both stretched out on the beds. "I'm too excited to sleep," Anna said. "I love being in the circus so much. It's all I think about."

"I wish you could stay in the circus and travel with us," said Crystal.

"Me too," said Anna.

Crystal sat up and faced Anna. "Maybe you could, Anna," she said. "Jenny said you're a good clown. You could live with us and sleep right there in my sister's bed."

"Would your parents let me?" asked Anna.

"I bet they would," said Crystal. "They both said they like you."

"You think I could really join the circus?" Anna asked excitedly.

"Yes!" said Crystal. "Oh, Anna, we'd have so much fun. And Acorn loves performing. He and Jumper could perform together. Jumper wouldn't be so lazy with Acorn around."

"I wouldn't have to go back to Wiggins Elementary," said Anna. "I'd go to the School Van. That would be so neat."

"Mrs. Rochester's a great teacher," said Crystal. "You'll love her."

Anna suddenly remembered the one thing that could keep her from joining the circus. "What if my mother and father say I can't do it?" she said.

"That could be a problem," said Crystal. "You'll have to ask them in the right way."

The girls talked about how Anna should ask her parents for permission to join the circus. But none of their ideas seemed that good to Anna. She had a big problem. Who could help her solve it? Suddenly Anna knew who could help her. Pam and Lulu. She needed her Pony Pals.

Anna and Acorn performed better than ever that night. When Anna went out front during intermission, a crowd of people surrounded her. She was signing a program for Rosalie Lacey when she saw Pam and

Lulu coming toward her. Rosalie Lacey was six years old and a good friend of the Pony Pals. Rosalie loved Acorn.

"I ride Acorn," Rosalie told the kids getting Anna's autograph. "Acorn and I are neighbors."

"Can I have *your* autograph?" a little kid asked Rosalie.

"Sure," said Rosalie. The Pony Pals exchanged a smile. They all liked Rosalie.

"You were even better tonight than last night," Lulu told Anna.

"My brother and sister couldn't stop laughing," said Pam. "They'll probably want your autograph, too."

Anna pulled Pam and Lulu away from the kids. "Listen," she said. "I want to join the circus. But I know my parents aren't going to like the idea. They won't want me to leave home. I need your help. We've got to come up with three ideas."

"You're going to leave Wiggins?" exclaimed Pam.

"I have to if I want to be in the circus," said Anna.

"But we start school on Monday," said Lulu.

A little boy pulled on Anna's pant leg. A man was standing next to him. "My son would like to have his picture taken with you," the boy's father said.

Anna moved closer to the little boy and posed for the photo. She looked over at Lulu and Pam. "Can you meet me at the diner for breakfast tomorrow?" she asked.

"We can talk about it on the way home," said Pam.

"Acorn and I aren't going home tonight," Anna said. "We're staying here."

The man waved a hand at Anna. "If you could just look this way, miss," he said.

Anna smiled for the camera. The boy's father snapped the picture. The band started to play. Intermission was over. Jenny came up to Anna. "Anna, help me move the people back into the tent," she said.

"I'll see you tomorrow morning," Anna called to Pam and Lulu. "At nine. At the diner." Then she ran over to a group of people and did a cartwheel in front of them. "Let's go to the circus," Anna said cheerfully. "It's time to see The Amazing Flying Frenzis."

After the audience returned to their seats in the tent, Anna went out back to see Acorn. She told him he'd be sleeping in the circus stall that night. "We might join the circus," she told her pony. She pointed to the School Van. "I'd be going to school right there," she said. "I could see you from the window." Acorn nudged Anna's shoulder affectionately.

Anna looked up at the night sky. She noticed a bright star. "Star light, star bright," she whispered. "The first star I see tonight. I wish I may, I wish I might, have the wish I wish tonight. *I wish with all my heart that my parents will let me join the circus.*"

No Ideas

The following morning, Anna rode Acorn over to Off-Main Diner. Lightning and Snow White were not at the hitching post. Anna guessed that her friends weren't there yet. She tied Acorn to the post and went inside to wait for them.

Anna's mother was working behind the counter. "Morning, honey," she called out.

Anna gave her mother a big hug, and sat at the counter. Anna's mother poured her a glass of orange juice. "You haven't slept at home for two nights," she said. "I miss you."

"I miss you too, Mom," Anna said. "But I love being in the circus."

"I'm glad you're having so much fun before school starts," her mother said.

"The circus kids go to school, too," said Anna. She told her mother all about the teacher and the School Van that traveled with the circus. "There are only a few kids," Anna explained. "So it's like having a tutor all the time. A school like that would be good for me."

"That reminds me," Anna's mother said. "We need to set up your tutoring times for the school year. I'll call Mrs. O'Connor today. I thought we'd do Tuesdays and Thursdays after school. Is that okay with you?"

"I guess," said Anna.

Anna could see that it was going to be hard to convince her mother to let her join the circus.

"A little more coffee down here, please," said a man at the end of the counter. Just then Pam and Lulu came into the restaurant. Mrs. Harley went back to work. The Pony Pals made themselves bowls of cereal and banana and went to their favorite booth.

"I just told my mother about school at the circus," she told her friends. "But she doesn't know I want to join yet. I have to ask in just the right way, or she'll say no. I need help." It was time for three ideas. "What's your idea, Pam?" Anna asked.

Pam unfolded a piece of paper and handed it to Anna. Anna opened it. The page was blank.

"You gave me the wrong paper," she told Pam. "There's nothing written on this one."

"It's the right one," said Pam. "There's nothing written on it because I don't want you to join the circus."

"Why not?" Anna asked in surprise.

"Because I don't want you to leave Wiggins," answered Pam.

"I'd come home for vacations," Anna said.

"I don't think you should join the circus, either," said Lulu. "If Acorn leaves, Snow White will lose her stablemate. She'll be lonely."

"Did you know that Snow White ran away again last night?" asked Pam.

"No," said Anna. She felt frightened. Had something awful happened to Snow White? Anna stood up and looked out the window. Snow White was at the hitching post with Acorn and Lightning. "But you found her and she didn't get hurt," she said.

"She could have been hurt or killed," said Pam.

"She missed Acorn so much that she jumped the fence," said Lulu. "She wanted to be with him."

"She could have been hit by a car," said Pam. "Or been lost again."

"My grandmother saw her on Main Street," said Lulu. "We caught her just in time."

"We can find another stablemate for

Snow White," said Anna. "I'll help you. We'll make a poster. Snow White will like a new pony as much as she likes Acorn."

"That's a terrible thing to say, Anna," said Pam.

"Why?" said Anna. "Everyone knows that a pony can get used to a new stable-mate. Look how fast Acorn got used to the liberty horses."

"But Acorn and Snow White are best friends," said Lulu.

"And *we're* supposed to be best friends," Pam added. "Remember?"

"We can still be friends when I join the circus," said Anna.

"It won't be the same," said Pam. "We won't be Pony Pals anymore."

"You're going to go away and you don't care about how anybody else feels," said Lulu.

"You're being selfish," added Pam.

"You're the ones who are being selfish," said Anna. "You know how much I want to

join the circus and you won't help me."
Anna stood up. She turned her back on Pam
and Lulu and left the diner. They didn't
follow her.

Anna unhitched Acorn and mounted
him. Snow White nickered sadly as they
walked away. She seemed to be saying,
"Are you going to leave me again?"

Anna rode back to the circus fast. She
was angry at Lulu and Pam. She led Acorn
to the stall near the liberty horses. Anna
was sorry that Snow White had run away.
"But we don't have to worry about Snow
White," she told Acorn. "She'll have a new
stablemate. And we'll come back to Wiggins for long visits. I know you want to join
the circus as much as I do." Anna gave
Acorn an apple treat and went to look for
Crystal.

Crystal was helping her father wash
down the elephants. "Do you want to help,
Anna?" Mr. Landel asked.

"Sure," answered Anna.

Elly was lying on her side. Crystal was scrubbing her with a long-handled broom and Mr. Landel was hosing her off.

Crystal handed Anna the broom. "You do this part," she said, "and I'll put on the soap." Anna thought that giving an elephant a bath was the most unusual thing she'd ever done in her life. I can't wait to tell Pam and Lulu, she thought. Then she remembered. She was angry at her ex-best friends.

"Was your mother at the diner?" Crystal asked Anna. "Did you ask her if you could come with us?"

"She was there," said Anna. "But she was really busy. It wasn't a good time to ask. I had a feeling she would say no."

"Did Lulu and Pam have some good ideas?" asked Crystal.

Anna shook her head. "They don't want me to go, so they won't help me."

"That's not very nice of them," said Crystal.

"I know," said Anna sadly.

"Don't worry, Anna," said Crystal. "I'll help you. We'll think of a good way to ask her." Anna was glad that Crystal was going to help her. But she was still wondering, Can I solve this problem without my Pony Pals?

The Last Show

After Elly's bath, Anna followed Crystal into her trailer. Crystal's mother was cleaning up the kitchen area. "Hi, Anna," she said. "It's so nice having you around here. It's been lonely for us since Crystal's sister moved away."

Crystal and Anna exchanged a smile.

Anna had a feeling that Crystal's mother wouldn't mind if she lived with them.

"I like being around you, too," said Anna. "And I love being in the circus."

"We're having a surprise birthday picnic

for Mr. Chandler after the show today," said Crystal's mother. "You should stay for it, Anna. After all, you've been a member of the circus family these last few days."

"Can Anna's parents come, too?" asked Crystal.

"Sure," said her mother. "I'd like to meet them."

Anna and Crystal ran back outside. "That was a great idea to invite my parents to the party," Anna told Crystal.

"Your parents will see how much everybody likes you," said Crystal. "And they can meet my parents."

"We'll show them the trailer, too," said Anna. "They'll see that it's like a real house."

For the rest of the morning, Crystal and Anna practiced how they would ask the big question, "Can Anna join the circus?"

After lunch, Anna and Crystal groomed Acorn and put on his leg wraps. Next, Crystal went to her trailer to dress for the show and Anna went into the costume trailer to put on her makeup and costume. Then it was time to put on the rest of Acorn's costume. Acorn was restless and nickering when Anna came over to him. "What's going on, Acorn?" she asked. "Are you excited about being in the show?"

Acorn whinnied loudly. Anna heard a whinny answer him. She looked over toward Mr. Olson's paddocks. Lightning and Snow White were at a paddock fence. "Pam and Lulu must have come for the last show," Anna told her pony. "I didn't think they'd come because they're so mad at me." Acorn whinnied at his friends again. Anna put on his brightly colored harness and Acorn forgot all about Snow White and Lightning. It was time to be in the circus. Jenny came over and helped Anna hitch Acorn to the cart.

"It's another sold-out performance," Jenny told Anna. "Let's give them a great show."

"Right," said Anna. She stepped into the cart and drove Acorn up to the entrance of the tent.

The band blasted the first notes of the parade song and the circus began.

After their clown act, Anna cooled Acorn down, put him back in his stall, and fed him. By the time she finished, it was time to go out front for intermission.

Anna noticed that the ringmaster was talking to her parents. She wondered what they were saying to one another. Pam and Lulu came up to her. Pam held a big bouquet of flowers. Anna thought they were going to say they were sorry for the fight and give her the bouquet.

"This is for Acorn," said Pam. "It's made of flowers and grasses that ponies can eat."

"Thank you," said Anna. "I mean, thank you for Acorn."

"You're welcome," said Lulu. "I mean, he's welcome."

Anna felt weird talking to her friends when it didn't seem like they were friends

anymore. She was glad when a little girl asked for her autograph. While she signed the girl's program, Anna noticed that Lulu and Pam were whispering together. She wondered if they were talking about her. Anna handed the autographed program back to the girl.

"Thank you," the girl said. "You're my favorite clown." And she ran off to show her autographed program to her parents.

"Did you ask your parents if you can join the circus?" Lulu asked Anna.

"Not yet," said Anna.

Just then Anna's parents came over. "Honey, you're a better clown every time you go in the ring," her father said. "I am very proud of you."

"Do you know what the ringmaster said about you and Acorn?" her mother asked.

"No," said Anna. "What?"

"He said that you two were natural-born entertainers," her father said proudly.

"And that he just might take you into

the circus as a regular performer," added her mother with a happy laugh.

Anna couldn't believe her ears. The ringmaster thought she was good enough to join the circus. And her parents were talking about it! They were smiling. It wasn't going to be difficult to get their permission to join the circus after all.

Anna hugged her father and mother. "I want to join the circus," she said. "I was going to ask if I could."

"Are you serious?" asked her father.

"Yes," said Anna. "I've been trying to figure out how to ask you." She laughed. "I didn't know it would be so easy."

"But Anna, school starts tomorrow," her father said.

"Didn't Mom tell you?" asked Anna. "A teacher travels with the circus."

"Anna will practically have her own tutor," said Pam. "She'll probably study even harder than she does here."

Anna could hardly believe her ears. Pam

was trying to help her join the circus! Anna smiled at Pam.

Anna's mother put her arm around Anna's shoulder. "But if you joined the circus," she said. "I'd miss you too much."

"Anna will miss you, too," Lulu told Anna's parents. "But she'll have great new experiences. I learned so much when I traveled with my dad."

Anna looked at Lulu and mouthed the words "thank you." Lulu mouthed "you're welcome."

Anna was surprised by her friends. They didn't want her to join the circus, but they were still using Pony Pal power to help her.

Two little girls ran over to Anna. "You're a good clown," said a smiling dark-haired girl.

"I love your pony," said the other girl. "He's so cute."

"Can we have your autograph?" asked the first girl.

While Anna autographed the children's programs, Crystal ran over to Anna and whispered in her ear. "Acorn isn't in his stall. Did you put him someplace else?"

"No," answered Anna.

"What's wrong?" asked Pam.

Anna signaled Pam, Lulu, and her parents to come closer. She didn't want to upset the children who were waiting for her autograph. Anna looked at her parents and her Pony Pals. "Acorn's missing!" she whispered.

The Missing Pony

Anna handed the autographed programs back to the children. "I have to go now," she told them quickly.

"Mom, Dad," said Anna, "you look for Acorn in the parking lot. We'll check out back." Anna's parents turned toward the parking lot. The Pony Pals and Crystal rushed toward the gate and ran around the big yellow tent. Crystal was right. Acorn's stall was empty and the gate was open. The liberty horse trainer, Lydia, and her father were lining up the horses for their act. "Did you see Acorn?" Anna asked.

"I saw him in his stall earlier," said Lydia. "Isn't he there now?"

"No," said Anna. "I think he opened the gate."

"A clever pony could do that," said Lydia's father. "Jumper is always getting into trouble that way."

The liberty horses and their trainers headed toward the big tent for their act.

Anna imagined Acorn on the road trying to go home. What if he was hit by a car? Anna's heart pounded. She didn't care about joining the circus now. All she wanted was to find her pony.

"Where should we look first?" asked Anna. "We need a plan."

"I bet he went looking for you," said Pam. "I'll go around the other side of the tent."

"Maybe Acorn went to see Elly," said Crystal. "I'll check there."

"My parents are checking the parking lot," said Anna. "Lulu, you and I should check around all the trailers."

"We don't have to look for Acorn," Lulu said. "I know where he is." She pointed at Mr. Olson's fields beyond the circus backyard. In the distance Anna saw three ponies grazing. Lightning, Snow White, and *Acorn*.

Anna was so happy she wanted to hug her pony. "Let's go see him," she said.

"We'll bring him his bouquet," said Pam.

"They can all share it," said Anna.

"I'll go tell your parents we found him," said Lulu. "Then I'll catch up with you."

"Thanks," said Anna.

Anna, Pam, and Crystal ran across the field. Behind them they heard the band playing the opening music for the second half of the circus. The girls climbed through the rungs of the fence. Anna ran over to Acorn and gave him a big hug. Then she split the bouquet into three parts and fed the flowers and grasses to the ponies.

"He wanted to be with his best friends," said Crystal. "He missed them."

"The way I'd miss Lulu and Pam if I joined the circus," said Anna. She smiled at Pam.

"I asked my mom and dad if you could live with us," said Crystal. "They said you could if it was okay with your parents."

Lulu reached the fence and climbed in, too. "Did you find my mom and dad?" Anna asked.

Lulu nodded. "They're really glad you found Acorn," she said.

"Me too," said Anna. She looked around at Crystal and her Pony Pals. "I've decided not to join the circus."

"Yeah!" exclaimed Lulu.

"I'm so glad!" said Pam happily. "Your parents will be, too, Anna."

"Oh," said Crystal sadly, "you're really not going to do it?"

Anna could tell that her new friend was disappointed. "Maybe I'll join when I'm a little older," she said. "But for now I'm

going to stay in Wiggins and be a Pony Pal."

"My best friend is in a different circus," Crystal said. "We only see each other during winter break. You're lucky you can be with your best friends all the time."

"I know," said Anna. "I love being a Pony Pal." She ran her hand through Acorn's mane. "And I love Acorn."

Pony○Pals®

Be a Pony Pal®!

Available wherever you buy books, or use this order form.

Send orders to Scholastic Inc., P.O. Box 7500, Jefferson City, MO 65102

Please send me the books I have checked above. I am enclosing $_____ (please add $2.00 to cover shipping and handling). Send check or money order — no cash or C.O.D.s please.

Please allow four to six weeks for delivery. Offer good in the U.S.A. only. Sorry, mail orders are not available to residents of Canada. Prices subject to change.

Name_____ Birthdate ____ / ____ / ____
  First   Last   M   D   Y
Address_____

City_____ State_____ Zip_____

Telephone (   )_____ ❏ Boy   ❏ Girl

Where did you buy this book?   ❏ Bookstore   ❏ Book Fair   ❏ Book Club   ❏ Other   PP399

LITTLE 🍎 APPLE®

Here are some of our favorite Little Apples.

Once you take a bite out of a Little Apple book—you'll want to read more!

Books for Kids with BIG Appetites!

❑ NA45899-X **Amber Brown Is Not a Crayon**
Paula Danziger $2.99

❑ NA42833-0 **Catwings** Ursula K. LeGuin $3.50

❑ NA42832-2 **Catwings Return** Ursula K. LeGuin $3.50

❑ NA41821-1 **Class Clown** Johanna Hurwitz $3.50

❑ NA42400-9 **Five True Horse Stories** Margaret Davidson $3.50

❑ NA42401-7 **Five True Dog Stories** Margaret Davidson $3.50

❑ NA43868-9 **The Haunting of Grade Three**
Grace Maccarone $3.50

❑ NA40966-2 **Rent a Third Grader** B.B. Hiller $3.50

❑ NA41944-7 **The Return of the Third Grade Ghost Hunters**
Grace Maccarone $2.99

❑ NA47463-4 **Second Grade Friends** Miriam Cohen $3.50

❑ NA45729-2 **Striped Ice Cream** Joan M. Lexau $3.50

Available wherever you buy books...or use the coupon below.

SCHOLASTIC INC., P.O. Box 7502, 2931 East McCarty Street, Jefferson City, MO 65102

Please send me the books I have checked above. I am enclosing $ _____ (please add $2.00 to cover shipping and handling). Send check or money order—no cash or C.O.D.s please.

Name_____

Address_____

City_____ State/Zip_____

Please allow four to six weeks for delivery. Offer good in the U.S.A. only. Sorry, mail orders are not available to residents of Canada. Prices subject to change.   LAP198

THE Berenstain BEAR® SCOUTS
by Stan & Jan Berenstain

Join Scouts Brother, Sister, Fred, and Lizzy as they defend the weak, catch the crooked, joust against the unjust, and rally against rottenness of all kinds!

❑ BBF60384-1	The Berenstain Bear Scouts and the Coughing Catfish	$2.99
❑ BBF60380-9	The Berenstain Bear Scouts and the Humongous Pumpkin	$2.99
❑ BBF60385-X	The Berenstain Bear Scouts and the Sci-Fi Pizza	$2.99
❑ BBF94473-8	The Berenstain Bear Scouts and the Sinister Smoke Ring	$3.50
❑ BBF60383-3	The Berenstain Bear Scouts and the Terrible Talking Termite	$2.99
❑ BBF60386-8	The Berenstain Bear Scouts Ghost Versus Ghost	$2.99
❑ BBF60379-5	The Berenstain Bear Scouts in Giant Bat Cave	$2.99
❑ BBF60381-7	The Berenstain Bear Scouts Meet Bigpaw	$2.99
❑ BBF60382-5	The Berenstain Bear Scouts Save That Backscratcher	$2.99
❑ BBF94475-4	The Berenstain Bear Scouts and the Magic Crystal Caper	$3.50
❑ BBF94477-0	The Berenstain Bear Scouts and the Run-Amuck Robot	$3.50
❑ BBF94479-7	The Berenstain Bear Scouts and the Ice Monster	$3.50
❑ BBF94481-9	The Berenstain Bear Scouts and the Really Big Disaster	$3.50
❑ BBF94484-3	The Berenstain Bear Scouts Scream Their Heads Off	$3.50
❑ BBF94488-6	The Berenstain Bear Scouts and the Evil Eye	$3.50
❑ BBF94493-2	The Berenstain Bear Scouts and the Ripoff Queen	$3.99

© 1998 Berenstain Enterprises, Inc.

Available wherever you buy books or use this order form.

Send orders to:
Scholastic Inc., P.O. Box 7502, Jefferson City, MO 65102-7502

Please send me the books I have checked above. I am enclosing $_____ (please add $2.00 to cover shipping and handling). Send check or money order — no cash or C.O.D.s please.

Name_____ Birthdate ___/___/___
                                                              M   D   Y

Address _____

City_____ State _____ Zip _____

Please allow four to six weeks for delivery. Offer good in U.S.A. only. Sorry, mail orders are not available to residents of Canada. Prices subject to change.

BBS598